THE THREE WISHES

Once upon a time . . . a woodcutter lived happily with his wife in a log cabin in the middle of a forest. Each morning he set off to work singing, and when he came home in the evening, a plate of steaming soup was always waiting for him.

One day, he came upon a fir tree with strange holes in the trunk. It looked different from the other trees, and just as he was about to chop it down, the alarmed face of an elf popped out of a hole.

"What's all this banging?" asked the elf. "You're not thinking of cutting down this tree, are you? It's my home!"

The woodcutter dropped his axe in astonishment. "Well, I . . ." he stammered.

"With all the other trees in the forest, why pick this one?" scolded the elf.

Although surprised and a little scared, the woodcutter boldly began, "I'll cut down any tree I like — "

"All right, all right!" broke in the elf. "Shall we put it this way: if you don't cut down this tree, I'll grant you three wishes. Agreed?"

The woodcutter scratched his head. "Three wishes? Yes, I agree." And he began to hack at another tree. As he worked, he kept thinking about the magic wishes. "I'll see what my wife thinks," he muttered.

The woodcutter's wife was busily cleaning a pot outside the house when her husband arrived. Grabbing her around the waist, he twirled her in delight.

"Hurray, hurray! We're in luck!"

The woman couldn't understand why her husband was so elated, and shrugged herself free. Later, however, seated with a jug of wine at their humble table, the woodcutter told his wife about the elf. She began to picture the wonderful things that the elf's three wishes might give them.

The wife took a sip from her husband's mug. She smacked her lips. "I wish I had a string of sausages as well —"

Instantly she bit her tongue, but too late. Out of the air appeared a string of sausages.

"Sausages!" the woodcutter roared. "What a stupid waste! I wish they'd stick on your nose!" At that, the sausages jumped up and stuck fast to the end of the woman's nose.

"Idiot! What have you done?" cried the wife. "With all the things we could have wished for!"

The mortified woodcutter exclaimed, "For two pennies I'd chop — " He stopped, horrified to think he'd been on the point of wishing his tongue chopped off. Still, as he watched his wife bitterly complaining, he burst out laughing.

"If only you knew how funny you look with those sausages on the end of your nose!"

The wife tugged at the sausages, but they wouldn't budge. She pulled again and again, but in vain. The sausages were firmly attached to her nose. "They'll be here for the rest of my life!" she wailed.

"Let me try," said the woodcutter, feeling sorry for his wife while wondering how he could ever put up with a woman with such an awkward nose.

Grasping the string of sausages, he tugged with all his might. But he simply pulled his wife over on top of him. The pair sat on the floor, gazing sadly at each other.

"What shall we do now?" they said, each thinking the same thing.

"There's only one thing we can do," said the woodcutter's wife timidly.

"Yes, I'm afraid so," her husband sighed, remembering their dreams, and he bravely wished the third and last wish: "I wish the sausages would leave my wife's nose."

And they did. Instantly, husband and wife hugged each other tearfully. "Maybe we'll be poor," they said, "but we'll be happy again!"

THE HOLE THAT WAS TOO NARROW

Once upon a time, a stoat was so greedy that he would eat anything that came his way.

He found some stale eggs in a barn and, as usual, gobbled them all up. Soon he started to feel agonizing pains in his stomach. His eyes grew dim and he broke out in a cold sweat.

For days, the stoat lay between life and death. At last, recovered but weak, he tried to climb a tree to rob a nest. His head began to spin, and he fell to the ground.

Sick with hunger, he limped about in search of food. Finally, good luck came his way. Although wary of humans, he ventured near a tavern on the outskirts of a village. The air was full of delicious smells, and the poor stoat felt his mouth watering.

A particularly inviting smell came from a crack in the wall. Thrusting his nose into the crack, he was greeted by a waft of delicious scents. The stoat frantically clawed at the crack with paws and teeth, trying to widen it. Slowly the plaster began to crumble. Shoving with all his might, the stoat made a hole and climbed through.

What a sight met his astonished gaze! He was in a pantry full of hams, sausages, cheeses, honey, jam, fruit, nuts, and all sorts of good things.

The stoat couldn't make up his mind what to taste first. He jumped from one thing to another, munching until his stomach was full. Satisfied at last, he fell asleep.

Soon the stoat was strong enough to climb up to the topmost shelves and try the tastiest delicacies. By this time, he was just having a nibble here and a nibble there. But he never stopped eating.

"Now let's see," he would mutter, "cheese first . . . no, the ham's better! And I'll have a little bit of pickled sausage too." In just a few days, the stoat became so fat that his trouser button popped.

One afternoon, however, the stoat froze at the creak of a door. Heavy footsteps thumped down the stairs, and the stoat looked helplessly around. He ran to the hole in the wall. Alas, although his head and shoulders could fit through, his stomach simply couldn't make it. The stoat was stuck!

Two powerful hands grabbed him by the tail.

"You greedy little robber! Thought you could get away, did you? I'll soon deal with you."

Strange though it may seem, the only thought in the greedy stoat's head at that moment was a longing to be thin and starving again!

THE PRINCESS AND THE PEA

Once upon a time . . . there was a prince who, after wandering the land in search of a wife, returned to his castle and told his unhappy parents that he had been unable to find a bride.

Now this young man was difficult to please, and had not been greatly taken with any of the noble young ladies he had met on his travels. He was looking for a bride who was not only beautiful, well-born, and elegant, but who possessed the delicacy of a genuine princess.

One evening, during a fierce storm, a persistent knocking was heard at the castle door. The prince's father sent a servant to find out who was there. Standing on the steps, lit by flashes of lightning, was a young woman.

"I am a princess," she said, "seeking shelter for myself and my page. My carriage has broken down and the coachman can't repair it until tomorrow."

In the meantime, the prince's mother had appeared to welcome the guests. She stared disapprovingly at the girl's muddy garments, and decided to find out if she was really of noble birth.

"Prepare a bed in the Blue Room," she said to the servants. "I'll come myself to make sure everything is in order." She had them pile twelve mattresses on the bed, and under the bottom one she hid a pea.

In the morning the prince's mother asked her guest, "Did you sleep well? Was the bed comfortable?"

"Oh, the bed was lovely and soft," replied the girl politely, "so soft that I could feel something hard under the bottom mattress. This morning I discovered it was a pea. It kept me awake all night!"

The prince's mother offered her apologies, then rushed off to her son. "A real princess at last! Just think! She could feel the pea that I hid under the bottom mattress! Only a true princess would be delicate enough for that!"

And so the prince finally found the bride of his dreams.

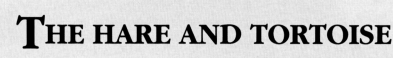

THE HARE AND TORTOISE

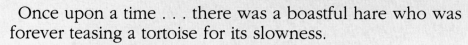

Once upon a time . . . there was a boastful hare who was forever teasing a tortoise for its slowness.

One day, the irate tortoise answered back, "Who do you think you are, anyway? You may be swift, but even you can be beaten!"

The hare squealed with laughter. "Beaten? Me? Not by you, surely! I bet nobody in the world can win against me. Care to try?"

Annoyed by such bragging, the tortoise accepted the challenge. A course was planned, and the next day at dawn they stood at the starting line.

The hare yawned lazily as the tortoise trudged off. "Take your time," he said. "I'll have forty winks and catch up with you in a minute."

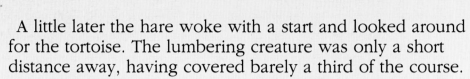

A little later the hare woke with a start and looked around for the tortoise. The lumbering creature was only a short distance away, having covered barely a third of the course.

The hare breathed a sigh of relief and decided he might as well have breakfast, so off he went to sample some cabbages in a nearby field. But the heavy meal and the hot sun made his eyelids droop. With a careless glance at the tortoise, now halfway along the course, he decided to have another snooze.

The sun had started to sink below the horizon when the tortoise, who had been plodding along all day, came within a yard of the winning post. At this very moment the hare woke with a jolt. The tortoise was just a speck in the distance. Away dashed the hare, leaping and bounding, his tongue lolling as he gasped for breath.

Just a little more, and the hare would reach the winning post first. But his last leap was too late. While he was still in the air, the tortoise ambled past the post.

Poor hare! Shamefaced and exhausted, he slumped down beside the tortoise. The tortoise smiled and blinked gently.

"Slow and steady wins the race," he said.

THE FOX AND THE GRAPES

Once upon a time . . . there lived a crafty, quick-witted fox in a wood. The rabbits, birds, and all the other small creatures fled at the sight of him, for they knew how cruel and hungry he was.

Since his prey kept fearfully out of sight, the fox was obliged to haunt the neighboring farms in hope of catching a hen or two.

Near a lonely peasant's cottage he found a poorly guarded hen run. "How careless of them to leave such tender, fat hens unguarded," chuckled the fox as he trotted away, licking his chops.

A few days later, he decided to try again. He crept up to the wall. A thread of smoke curled from the cottage chimney, but all was quiet. With a great bound, he leapt into the hen run. The cackling hens scattered, but the fox was already clutching one in his jaws when a stone hit him.

"Wicked brute!" yelled a man waving a stick. "Now I've got you!"

Up raced a large dog, snarling and snapping. The fox dropped the hen and leapt at the wall.

So frightened was the fox that he fell back, and could almost feel the dog's fangs sinking into his ear. Desperately, he jumped again and scrambled over the wall. He raced into the wood, yells and stones streaming after him.

"Bad luck!" he muttered, but hunger gnawed his stomach, and he looked around for a possible meal. Right above his head was a vine, laden with bunches of ripe grapes.

"Well, if there's nothing else . . ." he said, and jumped at the grapes. But the fruit was hanging just beyond his reach. The fox then took a running jump, but without success. Over and over again he tried, but the grapes always remained beyond his grasp.

"Caw! Caw! Caw!" mocked a passing crow overhead.

"Ha!" retorted the fox, disgustedly. "They're sour grapes anyway. Who wants to eat them? I'll come back when they're ripe." And he marched off on an empty stomach, thrusting out his chest to give himself airs.

THE ELVES AND THE SHOEMAKER

Once upon a time there lived a poor shoemaker. As he became old, he became poorer, for his eyes were weak and he couldn't work as well as in the old days.

One night, when he felt he and his wife would soon starve, he went to bed sadly, leaving a pair of shoes half done. To his great surprise, the next morning when he came into the workshop, the shoes were finished!

During the day, he set out all the tools and leather needed for a pair of shoes for a rich customer. "Tomorrow morning, when I'm feeling stronger, I will begin work," he thought.

But the next morning, instead of the leather he had left out the night before, the shoemaker found a beautifully sewn pair of shoes. The customer was delighted when he saw the shoes, and paid the shoemaker twice the price agreed upon.

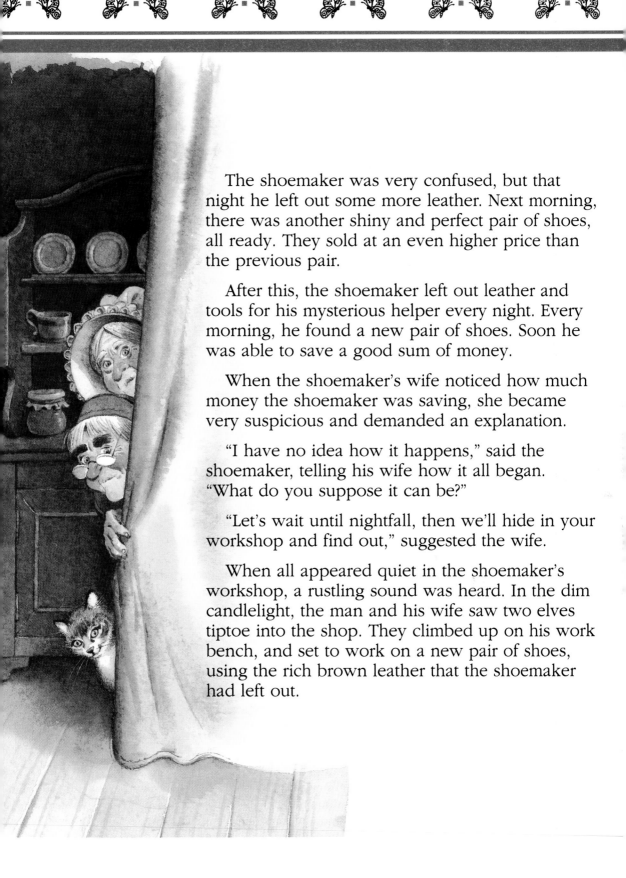

The shoemaker was very confused, but that night he left out some more leather. Next morning, there was another shiny and perfect pair of shoes, all ready. They sold at an even higher price than the previous pair.

After this, the shoemaker left out leather and tools for his mysterious helper every night. Every morning, he found a new pair of shoes. Soon he was able to save a good sum of money.

When the shoemaker's wife noticed how much money the shoemaker was saving, she became very suspicious and demanded an explanation.

"I have no idea how it happens," said the shoemaker, telling his wife how it all began. "What do you suppose it can be?"

"Let's wait until nightfall, then we'll hide in your workshop and find out," suggested the wife.

When all appeared quiet in the shoemaker's workshop, a rustling sound was heard. In the dim candlelight, the man and his wife saw two elves tiptoe into the shop. They climbed up on his work bench, and set to work on a new pair of shoes, using the rich brown leather that the shoemaker had left out.

How their needles and hammers flew as they worked! Their speed and skill astonished the shoemaker. Now he could understand why the shoes were so fine!

It was winter, and the elves were clothed in rags. They shivered as they worked.

"Poor fellows! They must be very cold," the shoemaker's wife whispered to her husband. "Tomorrow I will make them two thick wool jackets. That way they will be warmer and perhaps, instead of one pair of shoes, they'll make two!"

The following night, next to the leather, the elves found two elegant red jackets with gold buttons. They put on the jackets and began to dance for joy.

"We'll never be cold again!" they chanted in delight.

"Let's get to work now," suggested one.

"Work?" said the other. "What for? With two jackets like these, we're rich. We'll never have to work again."

And with that, much to the astonishment of the shoemaker and his even more puzzled wife, the two elves danced out of the shop. But although they were never seen again, the shoemaker prospered from that day forth.